Jack and the Beanstalk

Miles Kelly

Jack and his mother were very poor.

One day, Jack's mother said to him, "You must take the cow to market and sell her." They needed money to buy food.

Jack hadn't gone far when he met an old man who offered to swap **five beans** for the cow.

"Why would I do that?" asked Jack.

"These beans are magic. Plant them at night and by morning they will have grown right up to the sky."

So Jack took the beans and went home.

Jack's mother was furious.
"You've been tricked!" she cried, as she
threw the beans out of the window.

She sent Jack
to bed without
any supper.

In the morning, Jack looked outside in amazement. A huge **beanstalk** had grown – it went up and up, and up!

The beans really were **magic!**

Jack quickly got dressed. "I'm going on an adventure," he told his mother.

He began to climb
the beanstalk.

When at last he reached
the top, he saw a magnificent
house sitting on
a cloud.

Jack knocked on the door, and a giantess opened it.

"I suppose you're hungry after all that climbing," she said. "Come in and have some breakfast."

Jack had only eaten a little before the whole house started to shake.

"My husband is home," said the giantess.

"You must hide!"

Hastily, Jack hid. He peeked out to see a HUGE giant stomp into the kitchen.

"FEE FI FO FUM, I smell the blood of an Englishman!"

The giant searched but couldn't find Jack, so he ate a huge breakfast, then started to count his gold.

He soon fell fast asleep.

Jack snatched a bag of gold and dashed out of the house and down the beanstalk.

His mother was so pleased to see him. And now they had money for food!

The next day, Jack climbed the beanstalk again. The giantess let him in, and her husband was soon home. Again, Jack hid.

"FEE FI FO FUM, I smell the blood of an Englishman!"

After his breakfast, the giant placed a **golden hen** on the table.

"Lay, hen!" he ordered, and the hen started laying golden eggs.

When the giant fell asleep, Jack snatched the hen and climbed down the beanstalk.

His mother was delighted.

Jack climbed the beanstalk
again the next day.
He crept into
the house.

He knew the giantess
would not have let
him in again.

Then the giant placed a golden harp on the table. "Play, harp!" he said.

The harp began playing a beautiful lullaby. Soon the giant was snoring.

Jack snatched the harp
and raced out of the
house and back down
the beanstalk.

But the harp called,
"Master, master!"
and the giant woke up.

The giant chased Jack
down the beanstalk.
"FEE FI FO FUM!
I SMELL THE
BLOOD OF AN
ENGLISHMAN!"

As Jack reached the bottom, he ran to fetch an axe.

He chopped and chopped until...

CRASH!

The giant was flung
far away, and Jack
never saw him again.

The beanstalk
tumbled to the
ground.

Jack and his mother lived happily ever after, and were never poor again.